The next time you see a steamroller doing that, look and see if Mr Slow is driving it.

If he is, you shout to him, "Hello, Mr Slow! Are you having a nice time?"

And he'll wave, and shout back to you.

"Yes … thank … you … Good … bye!"

But then, Mr Happy had an extremely good idea.

Most sensible.

"Be a steamroller driver," he suggested.

And today that is exactly what Mr Slow does.

Slowly backwards and slowly forwards he drives.

Up and down.

Down and up.

Ever so slowly.

Can you imagine?

No! No! No!

"Be a speedboat driver!" suggested Mr Tickle.

Can you imagine?

No! No!

"Be an engine driver!" suggested Mr Funny.

Can you imagine?

No!

Poor Mr Slow.

He went around to ask the other Mr Men what he should do.

"Be a racing driver!" suggested Mr Silly.

So, Mr Slow got himself a job making woolly scarves. But, by the time he'd finished making the scarves, it wasn't exactly the right sort of weather to be selling scarves!

Phew!

And, that summer, Mr Slow got a job making ice cream. But, by the time he'd made the ice cream, it wasn't exactly the right sort of weather to be selling ice cream!

Brrrr!

Then, Mr Slow got himself a job as a taxi driver.

"Take me to the railway station," cried Mr Uppity, as he leapt into his taxi. "I have a train to catch at three o'clock!"

"Right … ho," said Mr Slow, and set off.

At one mile an hour!

And arrived at the station at four o'clock.

So, that job wasn't any good.

Was it?

"Good … evening …," said Mr Slow. "Here … is … the … nine … o' … clock … news."

It took him until midnight to read it!

And everybody who was watching went to sleep.

So, that job wasn't any good.

Was it?

Now, this story isn't about the time Mr Slow went on a picnic with Mr Busy.

That's another story.

No, this story is about the time Mr Slow decided to get a job.

He read all the job advertisements in the Sunday paper (which took him until Wednesday), and then he went and got himself a job reading the news on television.

Can you imagine?

It was very embarrassing!

For instance.

Last Christmas, it took Mr Slow until New Year's Eve to open his Christmas presents.

And then it took him until Easter to write his thank-you letters!

Oh, he was a slow man.

For instance.

If Mr Slow was eating a currant cake for tea, it took him until bedtime.

He'd eat it crumb by crumb, currant by currant, chewing each crumb and each currant one hundred times.

For instance.

If Mr Slow was writing this book about himself, you wouldn't be able to read it yet.

He wouldn't even have got as far as this page!

And, as you might well know, or maybe you don't, Mr Slow talked in an extraordinarily slow way.

He … talked … like … this.

And every single thing he did was as slow as the way he talked.

Mr Slow, as you might well know, or maybe you don't, lived next door to Mr Busy.

He'd built his house himself.

Slowly.

It had taken him ten years!

MR. SLOW

by Roger Hargreaves

EGMONT